Mr. Drumlin's
Orchard

Mr. Drumlin's Orchard

Keith Weaver

IGUANA

Editor: Lee Parpart
Front cover photo – Green Man carving: courtesy of Shutterstock.com
Front cover photo – orchard: by Liana Mikah via Unsplash.com
Front cover design: Daniella Postavsky

ISBN 978-1-77180-297-0 (paperback)
ISBN 978-1-77180-298-7 (epub)
ISBN 978-1-77180-299-4 (Kindle)

This is an original print edition of *Mr. Drumlin's Orchard.*

Dedicated to the young person in each of us.

One

It was August 22.

I had to be careful. If either of my parents saw me staring at the calendar on the wall, next to the old refrigerator, they would wonder what I was up to. I didn't want them to be wondering.

It took me a while to work out what the calendar was saying, but I got there eventually. I expected that August 31 would be the important date. Just how I knew that I'm not sure, but it was now only nine days away. I had also worked out that August 31 was a Thursday. Not that that made any difference.

All the information I needed would be posted on the village notice board. I didn't know exactly when it would show up, and I was aware, somehow, perhaps from one of my friends, that some years it disappeared and then reappeared a few days later.

There were four of us in our family: my father, my mother, me, and my baby brother Charles. My parents had picked up Charles only six months earlier at the place where mothers and fathers pick up new babies. They had gone to the same place to pick me up a little less than eight years earlier.

Our family was happy. I was happy because my father smiled at me a lot, because there were all sorts of birds in the trees behind our house, and because I had my lovely red bicycle.

I had two friends in the village, Henry and Billy. We were best friends. We had fun together — mostly. We went everywhere together on our bicycles. We swam in the river. Sometimes we fished. We played kick-the-can with other kids in the village. And we had bicycle races in the old abandoned sand pit just north of the village. We'd been friends since first grade, and we got along pretty well. But it bothered me sometimes that they seemed to want to do things just because they were things their parents had told them not to do. That made no sense to me, and whenever I said that I wouldn't do what they suggested, Henry and Billy both called me names. I didn't like being called names, so when that happened, I just got on my bike and rode off. I think they were a little surprised by that. But my world was bigger than just Henry and Billy. Most of the time we were friends, and we laughed and joked a lot.

From as early as I can remember, it seemed to me that I was lucky, that my family was lucky, and that in some ways things were special for us. There was our location, for one thing. Our house sat on the top of a ridge. Behind our house was a large vegetable garden that my mother kept, and behind the garden was a rocky ledge. From that ledge, I could look out over the village, and I could see where Henry and Billy lived. This was something special because I knew that neither of them could see where I lived from either of their houses. It wasn't that I was better than Henry and Billy. Just that I was lucky.

From the same ledge I could also see the large, rounded hill where Mr. Drumlin lived. The hill had a very nice shape, and was covered in thick grass. Just grass. Well, except for the orchard. In spring, there were blue flowers on most of the large hill. In summer, the grass looked very green and smooth and cool, and on summer evenings one side of the hill would be in sunshine while the other side was in shade. The sun and shade would move around as we got closer to night, and the sunny side changed colour. It went from bright green to darker green and then from pinky blue to purple, until the whole hill was just dark.

That year, when I was eight years old, I became quite interested in our vegetable garden, and I spent a lot of time watching my mother plant rows of seeds. After digging a small trench and sprinkling seeds into it, or poking holes for individual seeds, she would cover the seeds with earth and then attach the seed packets to little wooden pegs and place them at the ends of the rows to show where the peas, beans, lettuce, carrots, onions, radishes, and beets had been planted. A bit earlier that year, we had collected a lot of rhubarb from our garden. I guess my mother noticed me looking at the garden and the rows of vegetables, seeing the little green shoots come out of the ground, then seeing them turn into very different shapes of leaves. It was on one warm day in May that I became aware of my mother watching me closely as I stood holding an armful of rhubarb she had cut.

"You like the garden, don't you?"

"Yes, I do."

"Why?"

"Because these things all look so good, and because there are so many nice smells in the garden", I said, before burying my face in the armful of rhubarb. "And because … I'm not sure … because all this good stuff just seems to come out of nowhere."

My mother looked at me a long time.

"What an interesting thing to say!"

"Well, it does, doesn't it?" I replied, not wanting to think that my mother was contradicting me, or perhaps hoping that she would explain something I had missed.

"Yes. It does. Sort of. The seeds have the secrets for the different vegetables. All they need is soil and water. Once they have those things, they know what to do, and then we have vegetables."

"Do the vegetables know that we look after them?"

"I don't know. Maybe."

"Do the vegetables know that we will kill them and eat them?"

My mother gave me a long and very strange look.

"I don't know", she said finally, taking a long look at the garden. "I don't know just what vegetables know."

"Do vegetables really know things?"

"Oh, yes. I'm sure they do. But I don't know what."

I spent a lot of time thinking about vegetables that year, and a lot of time watching them grow in the garden, and wondering what they knew, and how I could find out what they knew. By the end of June, it was quite clear that each row of vegetables was different from all the others, and I was quite sure that the vegetables knew a lot, and that if only they could speak...

The village notice board was pretty much what you'd expect: a large square piece of wood held on two posts sunk into the ground. It stood all alone on a small patch of grass next to the drugstore, its surface covered in pieces of paper of all different sizes and colours. Each day, I rode my bike into the village, watched the same men who were always fishing from the dock, said hello to Henry and Billy if I saw them, and checked the notice board. Every day I looked for my special notice. And day after day, it wasn't there. Then, finally, on August 24, I stood under the notice board and saw a plain sheet of white paper with a message written in neat letters. It read:

August 31
Mr. Drumlin invites all children (and parents) to collect fruit and vegetables.
Noon to 4 p.m.

Two days later, on August 26, the notice disappeared. The day after that, on August 27, it was there again.

I knew that I wanted to go. But I also knew that if I asked my father, he would say that I wasn't going. For some reason, he didn't trust Mr. Drumlin. I asked him why, but all he would say was that Mr. Drumlin was a strange man. I knew better than to argue with my father. But as August 31 came closer, I became more and more anxious and concerned.

Deep down, I knew why I was becoming concerned.

It was because I was about to do something that my father didn't want me to do, and I wasn't going to tell him about it beforehand.

Two

There were large fluffy clouds in the sky on the morning of August 25. I finished my breakfast and then told my mother I was going to explore the buttercup field. Well, that's what I called it. Because it was full of buttercups. My mother knew it as the large meadow on Mr. Howell's abandoned farm, and she warned me, as she always did, not to play in the old barn. In fact, I was going to the buttercup field, but I wasn't going to explore it. I was going there to think.

There were thousands of buttercups. There were also a few small grass snakes, and a garter snake, and although they always made me shiver a bit when I first saw them, I knew that they were just little animals and that they wouldn't hurt me. I always hoped that they knew I wouldn't hurt them either, especially the little grass snakes.

My plan was not well-developed. It mostly involved trying to answer questions that occurred to me.

Why did Mr. Drumlin invite people to take his fruit and vegetables?

I didn't know.

Did he have too many to use himself?

Probably.

Did he want company? Was he lonely?

I didn't know. Possibly.

Why did people seem not to like him, or at least why did they seem not to trust him?

Again, not sure. Could it be because he was different? I tried to think of other people who were different. There was Bobby Macdonald. He smoked a pipe, and his drool ran down the stem and dripped off, and he was always talking about his chickens. But instead of not trusting him, people just seemed to think that Bobby was odd and harmless.

So, what was the difference?

My questions were coming to me more easily now, and it felt as though, somehow, I was uncovering some important secrets about the world.

There was one big difference between Bobby and Mr. Drumlin. It seemed that Bobby was always somewhere in the village — in the post office, at the bank, outside the barber shop — and he was always talking, sometimes even when there was nobody there to listen. He even started talking to me once. I said 'yes' and 'no' a couple of times, then just slipped away. He didn't even seem to notice when I was no longer there. He just kept on talking.

But Mr. Drumlin — he was different in a different sort of way.

I couldn't remember seeing Mr. Drumlin in town much, or at least not the way I remembered seeing Bobby there. Mr. Drumlin would sometimes come out of the hardware store, usually carrying a small bag of things that clinked, and if anyone looked at him, he wouldn't say anything, but he would touch the old gray hat he always wore. He didn't smile, but he didn't frown either.

Did people think of him in that uncertain way just because he wasn't friendly enough?

And what about Sam? Everyone said Sam was Mr. Drumlin's friend, but they always pronounced the word 'friend' a bit oddly. Sam was a white-haired lady who lived alone in a small cottage not far from the old railway station. I never saw this happen, but I heard people say that Mr. Drumlin would walk the quarter mile from his place to Sam's cottage every

Friday afternoon, and that they would walk back to Mr. Drumlin's place together. Then at about ten o'clock in the evening, Mr. Drumlin would walk her back to her cottage.

How, I wondered, was that different from Jim Richards and Mrs. Crosby, whose husband had died? They met most afternoons and sat on one of the benches in the little park next to the river. But, I said to myself in a moment of discovery, I had seen them, and they talked to everyone who passed by.

Why should this matter? I asked myself. There were plenty of times when I wanted to be alone. Did that make me odd, or did it mean that when I was big, in four or five years, that people would think I was strange, like Mr. Drumlin?

On the day I was asking myself all these questions, I was sitting on the trunk of a fallen tree. Daisies and buttercups waved in the breeze all around me. I noticed a small grass snake not five feet away, and I supposed that it hadn't been scared off because I was so busy thinking that I hadn't moved. The snake seemed to know that I was now awake, and it slipped away in the grass. But I had got somewhere in my thinking. I understood later that what I had just done was 'reach a conclusion.' I now knew that I had to find out about

Mr. Drumlin for myself. That meant doing what I knew my father would not want me to do, but what I had to do was too important.

One of the reasons I had reached my conclusion was that I had remembered something. Several somethings. I remembered hearing people talk at a hockey match in the arena about Bobby when he was younger. He had worked for the railway, and then he had worked at the plywood factory. His hair turned gray, then almost white, and he found an easier job helping Mr. MacIntyre in the feed mill. He worked there for quite a few years, then he stopped working and became just 'Bobby' who sat in the barber shop, on an oil drum in the garage in the middle of town, on the bench outside the post office, or on the stone wall next to the marina. Bobby loved to talk, and that's what he did.

But I also remembered people talking about Mr. Drumlin. One man who had lived in the village for more than sixty years said he couldn't remember Mr. Drumlin ever being any different. Another man who had lived in the village even longer said he could remember when Mr. Drumlin came to town, and that he did change over the years, but not very much. He said that nobody knew much about Mr. Drumlin. He would say a word or two, not more, about the weather and his orchard and garden, but he never said anything about himself. He wasn't rude, they said, but he would always find a way to avoid answering any question about himself or his house or what he did.

I'm not sure how I knew it, but I knew that people talked a lot about Mr. Drumlin. Only Mr. Wakelin would take Mr. Drumlin's side.

"You shouldn't say things like that about Mr. Drumlin", Mr. Wakelin would say, when he heard the rumours flying.

"Well, it's true", the other would say.

"No, it's not true", Mr. Wakelin would reply, "and you know that it's not true. You might not like Mr. Drumlin but that's no reason to spread stories about him."

When I thought about it, I realized that there was important information here. The information was that nobody really knew Mr. Drumlin, that Mr. Drumlin was a very private person, that nobody knew anything about Mr. Drumlin's past, and that somehow this wasn't right. At the time, I didn't 'know' it, in the sense of being able to say it in so many words, but at some level I was aware that some of the people in our village wanted to know about everyone else in the village, and they wanted to know quite a bit about them. If they couldn't find out what they wanted to know, they became suspicious and unpleasant. Many years later, I was able to examine this more closely and understand it better.

But then if Mr. Drumlin was such a private person, why would he want people to come to his house and help themselves to his fruit and vegetables? I couldn't answer that. But it seemed even more important then to go to Mr. Drumlin's place and try to find out.

It was then and there, in the buttercup field, that I finally decided that I would go to Mr. Drumlin's place on August 31.

Three

How?

How would I do it?

Having decided to disobey my father, I needed a plan.

I needed to reach Mr. Drumlin's orchard without being caught, and I needed to know what to do afterwards.

I started planning on August 25, the day after Mr. Drumlin's notice went up on the village notice board. That was the day I spent in the buttercup field. I knew that I needed to do a lot of careful planning.

The first thing I admitted to myself was that, after I had been to Mr. Drumlin's place, I would need to tell my father and my mother what I had done.

This realization came to me because of my new knowledge. I knew that some people in our village, perhaps most of them, didn't like or trust Mr. Drumlin, and that they talked about him. That meant that they would talk about who visited him and who he talked to. Following on my own logic, that meant that if I went to his place, they would probably talk about *me*. From there, it was a short leap to realizing that some of what happened at the orchard, including my presence there, would get back to my father.

I knew that although I would be in trouble for doing something my father asked me not to do, I would be in less trouble if I confessed to what I had done, rather than trying to get away with it and letting my father find out from someone else.

There were three other things that came out of my planning.

First, I knew I would need to go to Mr. Drumlin's place by the long way. That meant cycling up County Road 12, on the wrong side of the river, turning onto County Road 8, and using the little old bridge having curving circular sides, always known as the rainbow bridge, that carried County Road 8 across the river. I then had to cycle to Highway 14 and turn south, and that would lead me to Mr. Drumlin's place from the north. The direct route would have been to cycle through the village on Highway 14 and approach Mr. Drumlin's place from the south. But there were at least eight houses to pass if I went that way, and I suspected that some people spent quite a bit of time sitting by their windows watching what went on outside. Coming to Mr. Drumlin's place from the north meant that the only house I had to pass was Mr. Bailey's, and I knew from overhearing my parents that he spent most of his time at the far end of his property, in a clearing by the river, a long way from Highway 14.

Second, I needed to consider timing, and I thought my solution here was quite creative, and even a little daring. I would arrive at Mr. Drumlin's place long before noon, and try to leave before noon, so that anyone else coming for fruit and vegetables wouldn't see me there. Mr. Drumlin might not like that, and he might even send me away without any fruit or vegetables. That would be disappointing, but it was a risk I thought I needed to take.

Third, I needed to make sure that my plan would work. That meant that, well before August 31, I had to cycle the entire route along County Road 12, County Road 8, and Highway 14, but carrying on into the village instead of turning into Mr. Drumlin's place.

August 26 was a nice sunny day, not too hot, and at about nine o'clock, according to our kitchen clock, and an hour or so after breakfast, I set off on my bike. It was exciting, but also a bit scary, because I knew that I was preparing for something I shouldn't do. As I rode, I began to feel that there were eyes everywhere, and that somebody would follow me, or spy on me, and maybe even work out my plan, at which point word would get back to my parents. My palms were sweaty. I was nervous. But I tried to ignore all that and I kept going. I crossed the rainbow bridge, cycled up the long shallow grade to Highway 14, turned left, then coasted slowly toward the village. As I passed Mr. Drumlin's place, I limited myself to one quick glance, suspecting that 'they', the people who were probably watching me, would work out what I had in mind if I spent too much time looking at the orchard. When I finally rode through the village and arrived home, the kitchen clock said twenty minutes past ten. I guessed that it had taken me only about fifteen minutes to cycle from Mr. Drumlin's lane to our front yard. That meant that the rest of the trip had taken about an hour.

I had the information I needed now.

On August 31, I wanted to leave Mr. Drumlin's place by eleven o'clock at the latest, hoping that nobody else would arrive for their fruit and vegetables before noon. I thought that I needed about an hour at Mr. Drumlin's place, I knew I had to arrive there by ten o'clock, which meant that I had to leave home by nine o'clock. My bike had two large panniers on the back, and I thought they would be large enough to carry the fruit and vegetables that I would collect. I would show those fruit and vegetables to my parents as part of my confession.

My plan was in place. I thought I had good reason to feel proud of my advance preparations. Now I could just relax.

But I found that I couldn't relax. August 31 was still five days away. Maybe I had tested my plan too soon. Maybe I should have waited a few more days. Maybe my planning wasn't so good after all. Maybe…

The days dragged by. I could have spent time with Henry and Billy, but I worried that I might let something slip. They could easily have asked me whether I was going to Mr. Drumlin's place on August 31, and I knew that I wasn't a good liar, despite the carefully orchestrated lie I was planning to tell my parents. So, out of boredom and a determination to keep my secret, I did something else I wasn't supposed to do: I went to Mr. Howell's old farm and sat in the barn. That was on August 27. Although the animals were long gone, the barn still smelled faintly of hay and manure, but the air was cool, and a soft breeze blew through the many cracks and the spots where boards were missing. *What am I doing here?* I thought, alternating between depression and alarm. I'm not supposed to be here, yet here I am. Was I slipping into a life of crime? Would I be sent to reform school? Would my parents send me to stay with my horrid Uncle Stewie, who I was sure didn't like me?

But the day passed, and was cheered up by a rabbit that hopped into the barn, looked at me for a long moment, then slowly hopped past me and crawled through a hole into one of the old feed bins. Later I was cheered up by some swallows that chattered on the roof and in the rafters above me. The wind spoke to me. The old barn spoke to me. I thought I heard them telling me that everything would be fine, that I shouldn't worry. This was just what I wanted to hear, so by mid-afternoon, I felt a lot better.

Over the next three days, I found other ways to occupy my time. On August 28, I cycled to Taylor's Creek, to the spot where it passes under County Road 12, quite a long way after the junction with County Road 8. There are large flat rocks at Taylor's Creek, where one sat comfortably in the sun, watching the fish as they swam slowly upstream, stayed in one place, or drifted downstream toward the spot where the creek empties into Crow Lake. The fish were graceful, the water made a quiet gurgling sound as it passed over rocks, and the breeze occasionally brought scents from the trees that lined both sides of the creek.

On August 29 and 30, I dared to ride into town for a quick final check of the notice board to make sure nothing had changed. Both times, I saw the invitation and rode home to sit alone in the fields near our house. It had been days since I'd spoken to my friends, and a strange calm fell over me as I became more and more focused on what I was about to do.

Finally, after what felt like weeks, August 31 arrived.

I was up at seven o'clock, only a bit earlier than usual, not enough to cause my father or mother to be suspicious.

For an hour, I washed my bike, and then oiled the chain and the axles. I didn't want it to break down partway to Mr. Drumlin's place. When I had finished my toast and jam, I told my mother that I was going for a long bike ride to look at trees. She was making bread, and she just nodded and said that she hoped I would have fun. At nine o'clock, according to the clock in our kitchen, I climbed onto my bike.

My adventure was beginning.

The trip to Mr. Drumlin's place was just as I expected, and I smiled to myself at how organized I had been, and how well everything was going. The rainbow bridge seemed to offer a welcome to me as I crossed it. Highway 14 soon appeared. I turned left, and coasted slowly southwards. I could see Mr. Drumlin's place ahead.

All at once, I could also see something else. There were red streamers all along his laneway, and ribbons tied to several of the trees in his orchard. After passing at least fifty of these decorations, I turned into Mr. Drumlin's laneway.

But in making that turn, I would also encounter something new, different, unforgettable, and life-changing.

Four

I look around my library, a personal oasis, someplace where I spend a lot of time.

My father died twelve years ago at the age of 92. My mother died the following year at the age of 90. My younger brother Charles had died in a freak car accident when he was eighteen. On the death of my mother, the lovely house where my mother and father had lived all their lives — the house I grew up in — passed to my son and daughter, and they have used it extensively as a weekend retreat and a long-term summer home. The house is as loved now as when my parents lived in it, and I like to think that they know this.

Last year, I returned to my village for the first time in years. That visit took place on August 31, which is also today's date. In fact, each year on August 31, I spend a good part of the day reflecting on the events I put in motion all those years ago. That particular visit revealed some important things to me. It demonstrated that my connection to my home village was still surprisingly strong. It also brought back with some force the reality of Mr. Drumlin in my boyhood life.

But I need to carry on with my story as a boy of eight.

When I turned my bicycle into Mr. Drumlin's lane that day so long ago, and saw the many ribbons, streamers, flags, and other decorations fluttering in the breeze, the feeling I had was one of being welcomed. I parked my bicycle beside a large rain barrel at a corner of Mr. Drumlin's house, and then was uncertain what to do. There was a front door to the house, but it looked as though it was used only on special occasions. At the rear of the house was a large and solid addition, a very respectable shed, and a wide, squat door that stood ajar. The door had heavy metal hinges, a shiny knocker, and a long, cast iron door handle.

After finally working up the nerve to approach the door, I lifted the knocker hesitantly and made three little taps with it.

Almost instantly, Mr. Drumlin appeared. His face wore an expression of mild surprise, but cleared quickly when he saw me.

"Are you here for fruit and vegetables?" he asked in what I hoped was a welcoming tone.

"Yes", I said after a long pause. "I know I'm here early, and there's a good reason for that, and I want to explain, and I'm sorry if I … if it…"

"Please!" he said quickly. "There's no need to feel sorry. Come in! Come in! Or … would you like to look at the orchard and the garden first?"

"Yes please", I said.

We walked to the orchard. Mr. Drumlin explained that there were exactly 100 trees, 70 apple trees and 30 pear trees. I could see that they were all perfectly shaped and looked perfectly healthy, although I really knew nothing about fruit trees. There was fruit on each of the trees. The apples were bright red, and the pears were a lovely yellowy-green. The grass between the rows of trees had been cut with scrupulous care, and there was no fallen fruit anywhere on the ground. I thought of the apple trees that grew at either end of our garden. They had dead branches, a lot of the fruit had black spots on them, and there was always a scattering of fallen apples surrounding each tree. My mother picked up these fallen apples periodically, but I never recalled seeing our trees as perfect and well groomed as Mr. Drumlin's trees were.

We walked through several rows of the trees. Mr. Drumlin was smiling lightly.

"Are these the apples you'll give away to people who come today?"

"No, not these. I pick a few apples every day, when they're ripe. Those apples are in the shed. I'll give them away today. If anybody turns up."

"If anybody turns…? Why would people not turn up?"

Mr. Drumlin just shrugged.

"Well, we'll just have to see."

I didn't understand this, but something else had caught my eye.

"What are those lumps on the tree trunks down near the ground?"

"That's where I graft new tree stems."

My expression evidently indicated that I had no idea what he was talking about.

"Every two years, I cut off the trunks of ten trees, one row, just above that lump, and then I make a split in the bit of trunk that's left, and place a small branch of apple or pear growth into it, bind it up tight, cover it with something to protect the trees from diseases, and then wait."

"What happens then?"

"The bit of apple or pear growth begins to grow, and it grows very quickly. Within two or three years it is producing apples or pears."

"But why do you do that?"

"Because trees become tired when they get older. They produce fewer blossoms, and they produce less fruit. If I left them too long, they would become sick and die eventually. I want my trees to be healthy and productive. In fact, I want all the things I grow to be healthy and productive."

We walked around the other side of Mr. Drumlin's house, and into a huge vegetable garden. It was at least ten times the size of my mother's garden, and like the orchard it was perfectly maintained. We spent time looking at some of the rows of vegetables, and Mr. Drumlin explained what he was growing.

"Let's go inside now", he said. "You can pick what you would like to take home with you. And you can tell me what it is you wanted to explain."

The shed was much bigger than it looked from the outside. Along all the walls there were rows of bins, each bin full of apples, pears, or some sort of vegetable. The air was heavy with the rich, sweet smell of ripe produce.

"Would you like something to drink? I have apple juice or pear juice, freshly made."

I asked if I could try each, and Mr. Drumlin placed two glasses on a small table in the middle of the shed. I tried them both. I had never tasted juice that was so good.

"So. I'm curious to know why you came so early."

There was something I didn't understand here. Mr. Drumlin was friendly. He smiled. Not only did he not hesitate to talk to me, it was him who got the conversation going.

Even after all of my careful planning to get here, I never thought about what I would say if I was asked why I'd arrived so early. I thought of making up an excuse, but as I looked at Mr. Drumlin's open, friendly face, I just told the truth. I said I'd been curious, and that I wanted to see his place and meet him for myself. I tried to tell him politely about the people in our village, and how it bothered me the way they treated him. I told him also that my father would never agree to let me come here today, that neither my father nor my mother knew that I had come, and that I would be in trouble when I got home and told them what I had done.

Having explained all that to Mr. Drumlin, who just nodded at several points, I began to feel better, and I spent some time looking around the shed more closely.

My eyes had adjusted to the dark interior, which would have been gloomy had it not been for the colourful display of fruit and vegetables all around. This shed was a cheerful and welcoming space.

As I turned slowly to look at everything in the shed, I noticed a door leading into the house. Above the door was a wood carving of a man's head. Unlike any man I'd ever seen, this one had long, green, slightly curly hair, hair that looked like grass, or leaves. The carving was large, two feet across.

"Who is that?" I asked.

"Well, actually, that's me. I've made quite a few carvings of myself, and I think they look best when they're green. Do you like it?"

"Yes," I said, and the more I looked at it the more I did like it. "The face is smiling. You're smiling."

We stood for a while, looking at the carving, and I realized that we were smiling as well.

Mr. Drumlin turned to me suddenly, as though breaking a spell.

"I was just about to harvest some carrots. Would you like to help me?"

"Yes. I would."

We left the shed and walked along a well-tended path to the garden, where Mr. Drumlin led me to a row of vegetables that had lovely frilly leaves. He picked a garden fork from a rack of tools and waved me to follow him along the row of carrots. He sank the fork into the ground, pushed it back slightly, and then bent down and pulled a handful of carrots from the loosened soil.

"Go ahead", he said. "Now you pull some carrots out."

They came out easily, and the soil smelled rich and pungent. The carrots were perfectly formed, and even through their covering of earth, their bright, healthy orange colour showed clearly. We worked alongside each other, pulling more carrots out of the ground. Mr. Drumlin brushed them off gently and laid them in a wooden box he had placed next to the row. When we'd filled the box, we took it inside and left our load of carrots in the shed. Mr. Drumlin said he would clean them later.

That was when I spoke up about something that had only occurred to me while we were picking the carrots.

"I've never thought about it before, but your name is uncommon. Drumlin."

"My real name isn't Drumlin. It's Green."

"But why does everyone call you Mr. Drumlin?"

"That's probably because the hill here, where my house and orchard and garden are located, is a drumlin." He then explained to me what a drumlin is. He said he didn't mind being called Mr. Drumlin. It was only a name. And it wasn't worth the trouble trying to explain things and get people to use his real name.

I was suddenly aware that quite some time had passed, and I went to the shed door and looked out. There was nobody outside.

"It's now almost twelve thirty", Mr. Drumlin said. "I suspect that nobody else will be coming. Do you want to collect some fruit and vegetables now?"

I really wanted to stay and talk to him, but I knew that if I wasn't home soon, having left at nine o'clock that morning, my parents would probably start to worry.

My panniers were bulging. I said thank you many times to Mr. Drumlin, then asked if I could come back and visit another day.

His face clouded over.

"Well, I really only invite people here at the end of August. And if you get into trouble for this visit, would it be a good idea to visit again?"

He had a point, but I was crestfallen. There were things I wanted to know. There were things about Mr. Drumlin and his garden and his orchard, particularly his orchard, that were different, and that I wanted to understand. The orchard was perfect. And he had explained that ten percent of it was replaced every two years. That meant that the orchard was completely new every twenty years.

Mr. Drumlin's orchard was immortal, eternal. The thought was strange, fascinating, and somehow reassuring.

I went home. I told my father what I had done. He was very angry. He asked me many questions about Mr. Drumlin. I answered them all, and as I did, his anger seemed to dissipate a little, but he was still very displeased with me.

He looked at me, his expression hard and cold.

"I'm very disappointed that you did something that you knew I didn't want you to do."

Normally, I wouldn't have dared answering back, but Mr. Drumlin's friendly welcome, his generosity, and the unfairness of the whole situation, the unkindness in the village, made me just blurt it out.

"It was important. I had to do it."

To my surprise, my father chose not to reply. He gave me one more long look, then waved his hand, as though dismissing the entire episode.

The fruit and vegetables from my panniers went into our larder. We ate them all, but nothing was ever said about where they came from or whose work went into growing them.

I thought this was strange and somehow wrong — even ungrateful — but I didn't say anything.

Many times over the following weeks, months, and years, I looked out from the ridge toward Mr. Drumlin's hill, and thought about my August 31 meeting, and about the few hours I had spent with Mr. Drumlin. The images never left me — images of Mr. Drumlin, his unexpectedly happy and smiling face, his interest in me, his willingness to talk and to explain. I've never forgotten his beautiful vegetable garden, or the bins full of glowing, healthy fruit and vegetables, or the wonderful mixture of aromas in the shed.

And then there were the images of his exquisite orchard, his eternal orchard.

Five

In the years after I left home to study and then work, I visited my father and mother many times. Later, my two children, George and Kate, loved to visit their grandparents, as did my wife, Marianne. On the occasion of my father's eighty-fifth birthday, however, Marianne suggested that I visit them just on my own for a couple of days. By then, both our children had graduated from university and were working. They both expressed a wish to see their grandparents, but didn't insist when it became evident that I wanted some time alone with my mother and father.

As it happened, I arrived for that visit on August 31. It was close to my father's birthday (September 4), but he wasn't fussy about exact dates when it came to birthdays. I hadn't planned for that date; that's just how it turned out. I arrived at my parents' place early, before eight o'clock, and the three of us had breakfast outside at the picnic table surrounded on two sides by an unruly hedge of hazelnut bushes. After breakfast, my mother collected the lunch dishes, saying that she had things to do inside. My father loved walking, and on that occasion we walked to the buttercup field, looked at the buttercups, saw several rabbits, and encountered five grass snakes. I told my father about how I had liked grass snakes when I was a boy, and that I thought they brought good luck.

We talked about many things, my father and I. He was always interested to know how my career was going. By that time, at the age of fifty-eight, I had advanced as far as I wanted to go in the engineering consulting company I worked for, and my challenges had become a series of efforts to help younger people grow professionally. We talked about what my father and mother were doing. My mother had taken on the village book club and breathed new life into it. My father was now running the local Toastmasters, and was obviously enjoying it greatly. We didn't talk much about the future, except when it came to their grandchildren, since my father had made it plain, in his no-nonsense way, that he and my mother had come to terms with the fact that they had a very limited future.

They were taking each day as it came, he said — treating each one as a gift, and making it count.

Our visit had been going so well up to that point, and I don't know why I decided to stir the pot.

Out of the blue, I asked my father if he remembered my visit to Mr. Drumlin when I had been eight years old.

"Yes. I remember it", he said, smiling at the recollection.

"You were pretty unhappy with me", I said, but he only looked at me blankly for a moment.

"I don't recall being too upset."

I came close to contradicting him, but decided to let that one go.

"Have you come across Mr. Drumlin at all lately?" I asked.

"No. He's not there any longer."

"Oh! Did he die?"

"No. He moved away."

"Really?" I said in surprise. "I drove by his place today, and his house looks maintained and lived in, and the orchard still looks every bit as impressive, at least seen from the highway."

"A younger man moved in. I think it might be his son."

I thought about that.

"Did the people in the village ever get to know Mr. Drumlin? At all?"

"I think not."

"Did you?" I asked, after a longish delay.

"Are you accusing me of something, son?" my father asked, in a tone that was pure inquiry, without any hint of defensiveness or counter-attack.

"No! Not at all!"

My father was well known and well connected within the village, and indeed throughout the region. I had often wondered what he thought of Mr. Drumlin, and of how the rest of the village treated him, or at least how it seemed to me that he had been treated. Perhaps my father had his opinions but didn't air them. Perhaps he viewed the matter as one in which Mr. Drumlin had chosen what his life and relationships to others in the village would be, and that was the end of it. Or maybe he just had a better sense of the pulse of the place and felt that it wasn't his job to change anyone. I knew my father to be a thoughtful man, less given to prejudices than the average person, and generally concerned for the welfare of those around him, and I was more than a little interested during that last visit to know what he thought.

But I didn't pursue my curiosity on Mr. Drumlin and the village any further. We let the matter drop. That was the last time my father and I spoke about Mr. Drumlin.

Time passed. My parents died within a year of each other. In both cases it was mercifully quick, and there were no extended periods of suffering. In both cases, the loss I felt was acute and enduring.

By that time, my few acquaintances in the village were friends of my parents. My own friends and classmates and other people my age had all moved away, including Henry, or had died, including Billy. My son and daughter, who now owned my parents' place and used it extensively, had much more connection to the village than I did. That didn't bother me. My village life was now a closed book, and Marianne and I had very full and satisfying lives in the city.

I say it was a closed book, and that was true. Except for one thing, that is.

Mr. Drumlin.

For some reason, Mr. Drumlin never seemed to be far from my thoughts.

Marianne and I had just returned from a two-week stay in Nova Scotia, where we had chosen Wolfeville, again, as our base. That had been our fourth such visit, and Wolfeville was beginning to feel so much like home that we had already decided that our next visit there would be for a longer period, probably six weeks.

We returned home to the usual mixture of familiarities, threads to pick up, activities to resume, social events to attend, and a pile of mail to open. The mail consisted of the usual blend of bills, notices, and advertising, but there was also one plain white envelope, addressed to me, with no return address on the outside.

Opening it, I found inside a notice:

August 30
Mr. Drumlin invites all children (and parents) to collect
fruit and vegetables.
Noon to 4 p.m.

Who had sent this to me, I wondered.

But then, immediately, a flood of memories returned to me: the rain barrel, the decorations on the trees along the route to the farm, the old gray hat that Mr. Drumlin always wore, and the alluring mix of aromas in his shed all came back now with a force that left me stunned. I thought of the scrupulous order and tidiness of his vegetable garden, his systematic method for renewing the apple and pear trees, and the sweep of rich, thick grass that extended over the hill on which his property sat.

And then there was the orchard, which I could see again now, as clearly as if it were in front of me.

The trees lovingly pruned and maintained.

The apples red and unblemished and so inviting.

Mr. Drumlin's orchard. His eternal orchard.

At first I was unsure.

Should I leave the memory as it was, complete and perfect? Or should I yield to curiosity, travel to my village, and go to Mr. Drumlin's place just to — to do what? To see what?

It would no longer be Mr. Drumlin, of course. Perhaps a son was operating the place. Perhaps it had passed to other hands entirely.

I must have sat for at least an hour, that notice in front of me, pondering many things. In the end, I decided that I would go to my village and visit Mr. Drumlin's orchard once more. I called my son, learned that neither he nor my daughter would be using my parents' house that week, and arranged to pick up a key. Those decisions having been made, I marked the date on my calendar, stuck the notice on the cork board behind my desk, and moved on to the next important thing on my agenda.

But throughout the day, and over the next few days, Mr. Drumlin's orchard remained with me. August 30 was only a few days away, and I was mystified at the grip it maintained on my consciousness. As the day came nearer, I was astonished to realize that my sense of anticipation was that of a young boy, and that I was just as excited as I had been decades earlier when I visited Mr. Drumlin for the first time.

I travelled to my village on August 29, and if anyone told me that a smile had played across my face the whole trip, I would have believed them. I arrived in the village in mid-afternoon, bought the food I would need over the next two days, unlocked my childhood home and opened all the windows to air it, then set about preparing myself dinner: a ham and lettuce sandwich on thick-cut whole wheat bread, quartered tomatoes and sliced cucumber on the side, and a potato salad. I ate my dinner at the picnic table, of course, and noticed for the first time that my son or daughter had been pruning the hazelnut hedge in just the same, semi-neat fashion that my father had always preferred, maintaining the look of a bush that was free to grow as it pleased, but keeping it from encroaching on the picnic table. It looked exactly as I remembered it.

After cleaning up my dinner dishes, I wandered into my father's library. The shelf of old encyclopedias had been removed and had been replaced by about thirty children's books. But apart from that it remained my father's library. I recognized many of the books that I knew he loved and had re-read many times. My parents' love for each other, for their family, and for their lives, was everywhere in this house. Although they had been gone a long time, my own love for them both came back clearly to me now, as a gentle but bright flame that glowed inexhaustibly. Taking down one of the books my father had read at least ten times, *Tristram Shandy*, I settled into the big reading chair. At ten thirty, I rose, took the book to bed, and read for another hour. I was borne off to sleep on an odd current of combined reconnection and loss.

The next morning I woke early and ate my breakfast of toast, jam, and coffee outside at seven thirty. By eight fifteen, having had the company of many birds in the trees around me, I carried plate and cup back inside and washed them. I had brought an old, large, and well-used shopping bag to carry away the fruit and vegetables I expected to collect from Mr. Drumlin's shed, but the difference this time was that I planned to insist on paying for whatever I selected. As I headed for my car, my curiosity about what to expect at Mr. Drumlin's place was unaccountably strong, and it was with more than a mild tingle of anticipation that I made my way through the village.

From a distance, Mr. Drumlin's house and property looked no different than I had remembered, and as I turned into his laneway, I was surprised to see flags and streamers everywhere, very similar to the sight that had greeted me as a boy. There were no other cars or bicycles there, but then it was still only ten o'clock, and the notice had said noon to 4 p.m. I parked next to the rain barrel (of course), walked to the shed, and worked the knocker.

When the shed door opened, I must have made an odd impression. I stood there, speechless, in a state of combined shock and excitement.

"James!" the man said, smiling brightly. "James Whitlock, isn't it? Please! Come in! Come in!"

The old gray hat was unmistakeable, as was the face.

It was Mr. Drumlin, and as far as I could tell he had not aged a day.

Six

"Do come in, James!" he repeated at length, waving his hand in mock impatience and beaming at me his engaging smile, apparently unperturbed by the image of immobile stupor I must have cast.

"Or would you like to visit the orchard first?"

I managed to say that I would love to visit the orchard. Within a minute, we were among the hundred trees. The scent of ripe apples was overpowering in its gentleness. All the trees in the fourth row were saplings, indicating that they had been regrafted the previous year or the year before that. All the trees had that look of bursting with life — the apples large and firm and red, bunched together gregariously, and their branches bending under the weight of fruit.

It remained the perfect, eternal orchard.

I was so overcome by the impression of sameness and was so absorbed by the pull of this place, that I forgot my amazement at Mr. Drumlin's unchanged appearance. He talked about his orchard and his garden, and I followed him probably in much the same way as I had decades earlier.

We visited the garden, and it was also exactly as I recalled. Next to the garden, beside the east wall of the shed, there was a small sturdy table and two chairs. On the table were two glasses and a two-litre sized earthenware pitcher.

"I thought you might like to try some of this year's cider", Mr. Drumlin said, indicating that I should walk with him toward the table.

"I couldn't offer you any the last time you visited, of course. But I think it's particularly nice this year. There are far too many apples to eat just as fruit, and although I make apple sauce, apple bread, and apple pies, and I freeze dozens of those, there are still too many apples. Cider is a good alternative. It keeps well if I seal it properly, and in winter it provides such a nice reminder of summer."

We sat. Mr. Drumlin poured.

I still had said very little, but this seemed not to bother Mr. Drumlin at all. He continued talking as though I were an old friend.

We drank.

The cider was delicious, the essence of apple captured in every drop, and something else, too — something almost as timeless as Mr. Drumlin's orchard. Pinning down that something else was not easy. It included an elusive hint of the flavours and aromas of the fruit, of their necessary seasonal transience. But there was something else, subtle and persistent. A feeling of recurrence on a scale that implied permanence. Habit, ritual, and a type of social activity and function that returned year after year, century after century, were all tied in with this sense of an eternal presence at work within the world.

The morning sun beamed down on us. A faint blue haze emphasized the volume of air before me as I gazed down the slope of the garden toward the river. The richness of harvest time was everywhere. Luscious grass gleamed across Mr. Drumlin's hill. Swallows dived and swooped through the air. Thousands of grasshoppers croaked and rasped in the grass around us. The sky was a perfect fathomless azure, essence of ethereal lapis lazuli, a Sistine dome but far beyond the creative reach of any worldly artist.

I let myself be taken by the moment, gladly, feet on the ground, but at the same time elated, exultant. Mr.

Drumlin poured us each another glass. We spoke, and I was pleased that he had prodded me out of my silence, or the cider had, or the day had. We spoke of his garden, and he told me through an irrepressible smile how much he enjoyed the changes: turning the soil in the autumn, breaking it up again and planting in the spring, weeding, checking for pests, trimming some of the growth to find that sweet spot between abundance of crop and quality of crop, harvesting, and all the time watching the growth, development, maturation. And, yes, death.

"But your orchard!" I began. "Your orchard has always impressed me, right from the time I was able to ride my bicycle to the end of your lane and take a closer look at it. It changes through the seasons as well, but in a different way it's timeless."

We both looked at the orchard, dreaming in the sun of a golden mid-morning at the end of August.

"How long have you worked on your land here?" I asked, moving toward a group of questions I was no longer sure I wanted to ask, now that I had posed the first of them.

"Oh! A very long time!" Mr. Drumlin replied.

We drank some more.

"I suppose you know that I am not ordinary", he said in a friendly, conversational, matter-of-fact way.

Mr. Drumlin's statement took hold of me, being unexpected and hard to interpret, but at the same time awakening the sense of something both familiar and unknown, *quelque chose en même temps déjà vu, mais aussi jamais vu.*

"What I mean is that people in the village don't understand me, but I don't feel obliged to try to explain myself to them."

I looked directly at Mr. Drumlin.

"I'm not sure I understand you either, Mr. Drumlin."

He smiled, a smile of immense charm, and waved a hand, as if dismissing my uncertainty as a momentary bagatelle, something that would become clear very soon.

"If you think about it, James, I'm sure all will become evident. But now, another glass of cider, I think. It is such a perfect morning", and he poured once more.

I sipped as if in a dream.

"Let's go select your fruit and vegetables now, James. We probably shouldn't drink more since you're driving. Although", he continued through a giggle, "my natural inclination is to say to hell with it and be in the moment."

We rose and moved to the shed. The same aromas, that same intoxicating blended essence of fruit and vegetables that had left its indelible mark on my young memory, enfolded me once more as we entered. The bins were as I recalled, overflowing from the land's abundance. I pulled the shopping bag from my back pocket.

"Surely that won't be large enough", Mr. Drumlin commented in surprise, looking at what he clearly felt was my forlorn little receptacle. "Here", he said, as he reached behind him and took from a hook on the wall an immense cotton bag.

My objections were brushed aside. I selected from the bins as much as I felt was reasonable, even though it was on the excessive side, but Mr. Drumlin grabbed at least as much again from the bins, filling both bags to their brims.

"This is nature's abundance", he said. "Take! Eat!"

I struggled to move all of the bags to one spot near the door and was about to begin making 'time to leave' noises when Mr. Drumlin beat me to it.

"Another small cider for the road, hey?"

We returned to the table next to Mr. Drumlin's garden, where he poured us each about a quarter cup of the delicious golden liquid. We sipped companionably, and I wanted that moment to last forever: looking out over the garden, savouring that wonderful day, and imbibing the insubstantial solidity of the hazy, blue air.

I had been mesmerized by that eternal orchard for most of my life, and I wanted to go on being mesmerized, but at last, our cups drained and our conversation having reached a natural end, it was time to leave.

Reluctantly, I made my way back to the shed to pick up my bounty, and as Mr. Drumlin helped me load the huge volumes of fruit and vegetables into my car, I turned to face him.

"Thank you so much. This means a great deal to me. Thank you."

"Not at all, James."

We shook hands, his being rough, as I expected, from so much physical labour outdoors.

"I look forward to seeing you again, Mr. Drumlin."

"Mmmm." He nodded his head in a way that was hard to interpret.

And then I drove back to my parents' home.

It was still early in the day, not yet one o'clock, and I decided to start back to the city rather than spend another night away. I packed my things, checked that I had left everything as I found it, ready for my son's family who were due to arrive in two days for a week-long stay.

After locking up, I walked to my car, and was about to climb in when I noticed Mr. Drumlin's large cloth bag on the rear seat, full to overflowing with produce. Going back to the house, I collected five smaller bags, and filled them from Mr. Drumlin's bag back at the car, pouring the remaining contents into the fifth bag, rather than transferring them an item at a time. I would drive back to Mr. Drumlin's place and return his bag to him, with thanks. Behind all that there was likely the desire to take one more long look at his orchard.

When I turned into Mr. Drumlin's lane, what I found was not what I expected.

The flags and streamers were gone.

I drove along Mr. Drumlin's lane. The little table and chairs where we had had our cider were gone.

The door to the shed was closed. I tried the latch. The door was not locked, and I opened it and stepped inside.

All the bins along the walls were empty. The air inside smelled of shed. There was not a trace of the rich harvest aromas that had surrounded me here less than two hours earlier.

A forlorn feeling hung over the place, as though it had been deserted.

As I stood there, I became aware of a strong sense of sadness and loss threatening to overwhelm the feelings of wholeness and connection that I'd shared with Mr. Drumlin that morning. But there was nothing else to do. I closed the shed door quietly, returned to my car and drove back to the city.

It was a sombre ride.

Marianne was out, her note to me saying that she was at a planning meeting for the local horticultural society. I brought my bags of produce into the house and carried them all to the basement where it was cooler. Dealing with them would be partly a job for that afternoon. Placing the five bags onto my workbench, I paused when one of the bags, the fifth of the smaller bags, made a slight clank when it was set down. Probably just a tool disturbed when the bag settled on the bench, I thought, but when I peered inside the bag I realized that this was not the case.

In the bottom of the bag, a small face smiled up at me. It was about fifteen centimetres in diameter, and was green.

I recalled the large carving on the wall of Mr. Drumlin's shed, depicting a similar but much larger face.

An image of Mr. Drumlin came suddenly to mind. He really had not changed since I had seen him as a boy. He was the same age. During my visit, I had simply accepted this as fact. Now I wondered why I had not seen how strange and impossible this was.

I recalled also the feel of his hand as he reached out to shake mine when I took my leave.

His skin was rough, the hardened skin of a labourer. But there was something else.

His hand had a fissured feel to it.

It had felt every bit like bark on a tree.

Seven

I read quite a lot for pleasure. Both fiction and non-fiction. It's good for relaxation, but also for general knowledge.

And then there's specific knowledge.

Some of my specific knowledge came from my work. My focus for the large majority of my working life was on building and testing computer models. One of the lessons one learns in that game, and it can be a hard one, is that a model, no matter how good it is, is not reality.

The best model builders I know tend to be Platonists, meaning that they adopt the philosophically unpopular position of believing that what they are trying to model exists 'out there' in perfection. This approach, and especially the concept of a 'true value', an error-free value, makes some people jump up and down indignantly, but there's really nothing contentious about it. A good deal has been published on the various aspects of this approach, and it has been applied in some quite complex analyses and been shown to work. In that pudding is where one finds the proof.

At points in my life, quite apart from my work, situations have arisen where I've been forced to face the possibility that none of the explanations on offer make sense of what I see before me. In some cases, we just might not know enough; crucial pieces of knowledge might be missing. In some cases, however, the possibility has to be faced that the concepts and metaphors available to us are just too puny, or are not sufficiently comprehensive, to encompass the piece of reality in front of us and that we are trying to understand.

I felt I was being herded into that corner by my experiences with Mr. Drumlin. But there were a few things to check. The first of these occupied the rest of the afternoon: I busied myself doing a number of online and library searches. About 80 pages of printout from these searches kept me occupied that evening after dinner. The next day, I planned to travel again to my village. My objective was to speak to the oldest gentleman in the village, a man called Archie

Caroll. In preparation, I had been able to contact one of my son's acquaintances in the village, who confirmed, through a chuckle, that Archie was not on e-mail, but who promised to drop by Archie's place and ask if he would see me. An hour later, the answer had come back: Yes.

I drove to my village and found Archie in his modest but very comfortable bungalow. His clear, bright blue eyes and his amazing spryness seemed inconsistent with his 97 years. Opening his door to me, he beckoned me in, and immediately struck out for his kitchen, asking about "Coffee and biscuits?" over his shoulder. Five minutes later, we had settled down in his bright sitting room, some truly excellent coffee poured, and a plate of what looked like homemade shortbread and peanut butter cookies within reach.

"I knew your father", Archie began, before I had uttered anything beyond 'Hello' and 'Thank you'.

"Very nice man", he continued. "We both enjoyed walking. And I attended the Toastmasters for a couple of years. Didn't speak, of course. Crap speaker. Condition not curable."

We sipped our coffee, and in response to Archie's gesture, I took a piece of shortbread.

"What can I do for you, James?"

I gave Archie a stripped-down version of my interest in Mr. Drumlin.

"Drumlin, eh? Curious fellow. Very close with his words. Hardly ever said anything. Not at all unpleasant, though. I didn't understand why people took so unkindly to him. If a man wants to be left alone, then leave him alone. Don't try to do a Freud on him. But then there were, are, some very odd buggers here. It's nothing in the water. We had that tested. I put it down to the fact that the village doesn't have a library."

"What happened to him?" I asked.

"Don't know. He just disappeared one day. Not long after Sam Davies died. She lived down by the old railway station. He and Sam got together regularly."

"Did he come back?"

"Hey? Oh! No. Not as far as I know, at least. There was a young fellow living in his place for years after he left, but I never was able to speak to him. Son maybe? Nephew?"

"How long ago was that?" I asked.

"Oh! Years. Many years."

"And the young man. How long did he stay?"

"What? Oh! Still there, as far as I know."

"Did you know Sam?"

"Oh, yes. Knew her quite well."

"Did she ever say anything about Mr. Drumlin?"

"Nope. Never. Not a thing."

"When was the last time you saw the young man?" I asked.

"Oh! Well, it was just the other day. I go for a walk every day. Saw him coming out of the hardware store. Waved. He waved back. That was about it."

"As you know, Archie", I began, "I was raised here, and there was never a time I can remember when Mr. Drumlin wasn't around."

"Same with most other people, although I have to admit that most never paid any attention to him at all. Odd buggers, like I said."

"Do you remember a time when Mr. Drumlin wasn't around?" I ventured.

Archie gripped his chin in one hand, contemplating.

"No. Can't say as I do. And that's odd, now I think about it."

"He never seemed to age", I added, half posing a question, half making a statement.

"No, that he didn't. But then some folk are like that."

We talked more about the village, about how it had changed and continued to change, about some of the people Archie and my father had as common friends.

Archie poured more coffee and asked about Marianne. Eventually, the steam leaked from our conversation, and I stood, preparing to leave. Archie seemed to acquire a second wind suddenly, and began asking more questions, talking about the weather, and what a good growing season it had been that year, for almost everything.

"Mr. Drumlin had a very large garden and a lovely orchard", I said, when a brief lull appeared. "Did he ever sell any of his produce in the village? Do you know?"

"No. I don't know for sure, but I can't remember him ever having a stand at the little summer market. I would have bought his stuff. You only had to drive or walk past his place. Natural green thumb, it seemed to me."

"Do you know where he got his money?"

"Now, James. That's not a question you should be asking. Leave that to the old busy-bodies about the village."

I thanked Archie, we shook hands, and I left.

The trip back to the city was one of mental consolidation. I hadn't proven or disproven anything. But the number of possible answers to the main question in my mind had been pared down.

I now recalled Mr. Drumlin's direct comment to me: "I suppose you know that I am not ordinary."

That comment was beginning to take on a new meaning. I began thinking about things in a broader setting. I was now convinced that there was something here, and I wanted to get to the bottom of it.

Two days later, my son's acquaintance in the village contacted me again.

He wanted to let me know that Archie Caroll had died in his sleep.

Eight

The day after visiting Archie, I sat at my desk.

It was a week after my visit to Mr. Drumlin. The fired clay image of a man's face was before me. Hair or maybe tendrils of leaves stuck out generously from the image almost everywhere, and it was all tinged a green colour. I had taken it out of the fifth bag into which I had placed the last of the fruit and vegetables from Mr. Drumlin's large bag, and had brought it upstairs. I spent a long time contemplating it.

It took me a while, but eventually I found someone at the university who looked like she might be informed. The image looked vaguely medieval, and it was clear that I needed to inform myself, get some specialist help. About an hour on the telephone led me to the Department of Medieval Studies at the university. An appointment with a professor, who had been recommended, was soon arranged. At the agreed time, I turned up at her office, and tapped on the frosted glass door.

Marion Andrews was a tallish, slim woman, and probably in her mid-forties. She seemed to be full of the sort of energy that is just waiting to be released. Before leaving for my appointment with her, I had pondered what approach I should take. Presenting her something that sounded improbable, or mysterious, or just inexplicable would probably land me back on the street quite promptly. The best way seemed to be the simplest one.

She showed me to a seat in her small office, where we chatted for a few minutes before getting down to business.

Placing the fired clay figure on the table between us, I posed my question.

"I'm wondering if you could tell me what this might be?"

She looked at it intently, and, I thought, in some surprise. After asking and being given permission to touch the figure, she picked it up, turned it to look at the back, then tapped it lightly with one fingernail, seemingly lost in thought for a moment before speaking again.

"Where did you get this?"

"It was given to me", I replied.

"Did the person who gave it to you say anything about it?"

"No."

"Where were you when it was given to you?"

"Sorry? I'm not sure I know what you're asking."

"I mean", she said, "was it given to you here in Ontario, or were you somewhere else at that time?"

"It was here, in Ontario, just north of here. Why?"

She didn't answer right away, but then turned and pulled a binder off the shelf behind her. Opening it at about its mid-point, she flicked through the plastic sleeves until she found what she wanted.

"It looks very like a Green Man. Can I assume that you know what a Green Man is?"

"I have some idea", I replied, "but perhaps you could just make sure that I haven't got it all wrong."

"Okay!" she said, her eyes brightening as she leaned forward to explain. "The Green Man is typically a human face surrounded by foliage, and the foliage often is shown coming out of the man's mouth, ears, et cetera. There are literally hundreds of Green Man images across Europe, but the best-known and best-preserved ones are in England, Germany, and France.

They appear now almost always in churches, but the idea, the basic motif of a foliate head, goes far back, and ultimately disappears in myth."

I nodded to let her know that I was keeping up, and she smiled at me before continuing.

"There is a lot of speculation on where the motif comes from, but the trail is clearest from about the twelfth century onward. I've never seen a Green Man image this small before, but you can see", and here she turned the binder to face me, "that the images closest to the one you have are found in Devon."

There was a pause here.

"I'm particularly interested in this one", she said, pointing to the fired clay head on the table between us, "because I'm not aware of any Green Man figures appearing in North America. I'm hoping that you can get into the details of how you acquired this one."

The entire affair would seem so odd to someone hearing it for the first time that I wanted to avoid risking anyone's open disbelief. Saying anything about Mr. Drumlin most likely would have played right into this. "I can give you some details, but there's really not much to tell. It was … as I've said, it was given to me. That's about it. There was no explanation, no rationale. And I didn't know I'd been given it until I found it. But maybe you could tell me whether there is any way to determine where this figure was made. Could it have been made here? Might it have been produced in Europe and brought here?"

"It's small enough, it could have been made anywhere. But no two clays are the same. It's possible one might be able to trace it to its clay source, but that could end up being a massive job. A better approach would be to date it using the rehydroxylation process. If it really turned out to be old, and I mean in the range of 500 to 1000 years, then we would be safe concluding that it had been made in Europe. Why would you want to know where it was made?"

"Just curiosity, really", I said. I pondered for a moment, then changed the subject. "If there are that many instances of Green Men around, it must have been symbolic of something important at one time."

"Yes", she said, nodding. "But the best we can offer today is informed speculation. At one time it might have represented the oneness of people and the land. Tree spirits and tree worship were part of the human reality for a long time, and it might have something to do with that. Green Men are found predominantly at or near churches, since that was one institution that survived and preserved buildings, ornaments, and so forth. And its presence near churches might indicate that it was another of many pagan elements that was adopted by the Church. Green Men have been found associated with every phase of human life, including death. So perhaps the Green Man was viewed as some sort of woodland spirit that accompanied people through their entire life journey. There's a lot of speculation, but maddeningly few hard facts. There's virtually no written record on the Green Man."

"From what I'm hearing, it seems that you don't have too much doubt that this figure", and I waved at the desk, "is indeed a Green Man."

"Well, let me be clear", she said, back-pedalling delicately. "I've never seen a Green Man figure this small, and I've never seen an instance of a Green Man on this side of the Atlantic, so I wouldn't want to make any definitive statements without more information. And let's not forget that one can never rule out forgery. On the other hand, it bears so much resemblance to Green Men in Devon that if it isn't the real thing, it seems very likely that it was inspired by a real extant Green Man figure."

We both looked at the figure again for a few moments. It seemed as though there was nothing more to be gained.

"Well, thank you for your time, professor. This was very informative and helpful."

"Not at all. But could I ask one favour?"

My gesture indicated that she should ask away.

"Do you mind if I take some photographs?"

"No, not at all."

She reached to a folded tripod that had been standing in a corner of her office, moved it over to the desk, mounted a camera on it, placed a short yellow ruler next to the figure, then took about two dozen pictures, turning the figure through every angle, and photographing both sides.

A few minutes later, I was on my way home, deflated and unsure what to think.

I had learned something about Green Men, if not particularly about my Green Man figure, but those wisps of new information seemed to lead nowhere, open no new doors, cast no further light on the whole peculiar situation I found myself in.

Maybe this was just the end of it, I thought, wanting to believe that that wasn't the case.

Nine

It was a few days later, the weather warm and pleasant, and I was stretched out on a lounger in our back garden. The book I had been trying to read was lying on the grass beside the lounger, and I was adrift somewhere. Fair weather clouds floated above, and I was alternately warmed and cooled as the sun blazed or was obscured.

I had a lot to think about. I had related the entire affair to Marianne the day before, and not surprisingly she was puzzled and confused. We talked for almost two hours. She had many questions. My answers to most of them were an honest 'I really don't know'.

"Who is he?" Marianne asked.

"Apart from what I've told you, I know nothing more. He was always around in our village when I was young, and it seems that he's still around, or perhaps someone who looks very much like him."

"Is this some sort of hoax, or maybe a con?"

"I don't think so. I can find no basis for worrying that we're about to be cheated, blackmailed, or anything else. There's never been any hint of threat, or skulduggery. Nothing has ever been demanded. If there had been any suggestion of any of those, I would have walked away immediately."

Marianne was not convinced. She sat thinking and looking into space for a long time.

"What are you going to do?"

"Well, I don't plan to do anything. There's nothing to do, as far as I can see."

We talked a bit more. Gradually Marianne seemed to relax. I could well understand how she would feel. The whole matter appeared to be simply not of this world. And we tend to deal with that sort of thing by gradually blotting it out through denial.

Several other projects had intervened but were now complete and out of the way. My son had brought me a copy of a rather nice book produced by a local historian, depicting the roughly hundred and seventy-five years of my home village, and the previous day I had spent almost an hour paging through the book. There were the usual main street shots, pictures of the school and of churches, pictures of the river, of some of the first cars, shots in winter, pictures of muddy streets, pictures of horses and wagons, pictures of a group of men next to a large deer they had shot, pictures of people in twos and threes in front of the general store.

I drifted some more. Items to be done in time for the next meeting of the local historical society crawled sluggishly at the edge of my conscious mind. There was plenty of time to prepare for that; it was still ten days away. An image of Archie Caroll's face swam quietly up before me. He was smiling and saying that he could never be a public speaker. I continued to drift.

But I became aware, not slowly, but not suddenly either, that a cloud had settled over me. Which was odd, because I could feel the sun's full heat beating down on me. My mental state, my disconnected feeling, wasn't one of anxiety. Nor was it one of foreboding. It was a feeling of something unfinished, and something that should be finished soon. I tried to ignore it, but it wouldn't go away.

Without wanting to, without making any effort to do so, I remembered the flags and streamers the day that I drove to Mr. Drumlin's place. I remembered his big, charming smile and his old gray hat. I remembered the bins overflowing with colourful healthy produce.

I recalled the bins empty.

I recalled the sad, abandoned, airless scent of shed.

I could feel the roughness of Mr. Drumlin's hand, it felt like, it felt...

And then I suddenly remembered that neither Henry nor Billy had ever said anything about going to Mr. Drumlin's place.

And, equally suddenly, it occurred to me that there was never a time when either of them mentioned the poster on the village bulletin board...

And then, with a real jolt, I recalled one of the pictures in the local history book of our village. The picture was dated 1856. Three men, posing uncomfortably, one of them...

A powerful sense of 'back then and back there' came over me...

The free fruit and vegetables...

Was I the only child who...?

The hat. The gray hat. One of the men wore that hat. One of the men in the picture. It couldn't be! The man in the hat was...

I sat up suddenly on the lounger. I wasn't panicked, or anxious, but a powerful sense of urgency flowed through me.

"Can it be? How? Me? What do I...?"

Three hours later, I was still on the lounger. But I was no longer drifting, no longer just afloat, somewhere.

I was wide awake.

A large project had presented itself to me. No, not 'presented itself'. It had demanded my attention, imperiously, not to be denied. And I was already jotting notes on what I needed, how I would go about it...

There might be some travel. There would be a hell of a lot of reading. And there were a lot of people I would need to speak to.

Mr. Drumlin...

Had he come to our village, stayed about a lifetime, then left...?

Had he stayed away then for decades, only to return...?

Mr. Drumlin, or Mr. Green as I now recalled he had said was his name, had left a trail of hints.

These hints pointed to just one conclusion.

He was my Green Man, had always been my Green Man.

And I was convinced now that I would never see him again, not on this side of the grave.

Despite that, I had to know him. And that was my project.

But...

No! The rational urge to brush the whole thing off as a dream, something imagined, rose within me. I crushed it without a second thought.

Mr. Drumlin was real. I wasn't prepared to let go of that. He had left me a whole string of clues. And those were just the ones I had stumbled across. The belief was forming quickly that there would be other clues. They were out there, of that I was now convinced. My task was to find them. And they would lead...? Where...?

Never mind! I said sternly to myself.

I might never be able to meet him again face to face ... or however it was I had met him before...

But he was out there...

Now...

Somewhere...

Acknowledgment

As a sounding board, always there and always reliable, I acknowledge my wife Maggie.

Thanks Maggie.